James Mayhew
presents

# Ella Bella
## *BALLERINA*
~ and ~
# The Magic Toyshop

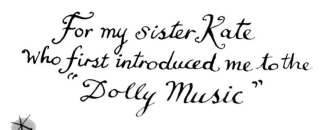

For my sister Kate
who first introduced me to the
"Dolly Music"

Many thanks to Antonio Reche-Martinez
for being the perfect toymaker.

First edition for North America published in 2017 by Barron's Educational Series, Inc.

First published in 2017 by Orchard Books, Carmelite House, 50 Victoria Embankment, London EC4Y 0DZ
Text and Illustrations © James Mayhew 2017

Orchard Books is an imprint of Hachette Children's Group, part of
The Watts Publishing Group Limited, a Hachette UK company.
www.hachette.co.uk

All inquiries should be addressed to:
Barron's Educational Series, Inc.
250 Wireless Boulevard
Hauppauge, NY 11788
www.barronseduc.com

ISBN: 978-1-4380-5005-8

Library of Congress Control Number: 2017935588

Date of Manufacture: July 2017
Manufactured by RR Donnelly Asia Printing Solutions Limited, Dongguan, China

PRINTED IN CHINA

9 8 7 6 5 4 3 2 1

James Mayhew
presents

# Ella Bella
## *BALLERINA*
~ and ~
# The Magic Toyshop

Ella Bella danced along the street to her ballet class. Her teacher, Madame Rosa, was waiting by the door of the old theater.
"Come inside, darling!" she said.

All the other children were
chattering excitedly on the stage.
Madame Rosa had put out her
magical music box, surrounded
by toys and dolls.

"Please may we play with them?"
asked Ella Bella.

"Why not *dance* with them!" said
Madame Rosa, as she opened the
music box.

"Oh, what funny music!" laughed the children.

"I call it Dolly Music," said Madame Rosa. "It comes from the ballet *La Boutique Fantasque*. The story takes place in a toyshop full of dancing dolls, all looked after by the kind toymaker."

"I'd *love* a dancing doll," sighed Ella Bella. "Would you love and look after it?" asked Madame Rosa. "Oh yes!" said Ella Bella. "I would!"

After the ballet lesson, Ella Bella stayed behind to tidy up. She saw that the lid of the music box was open and couldn't resist starting the music again.

As she danced around with one of the dolls, she noticed a door to a shop—a toyshop.

"Our first customer of the day," welcomed the kindly toymaker and his apprentice.

La Boutique Fantasque

"Oh, what a lot of dolls!" gasped Ella Bella, gazing at all their colorful faces and costumes. They looked almost real.

Just then, two families burst in
demanding to see the finest dolls.
"Which one first?" wondered the toymaker.
"I have so many boxes and so many dolls . . ."
He wound up a pair of Italian dolls with
porcelain faces. And they began to dance.

Next, the toymaker opened
a box and out danced some
playing cards.

Ella Bella opened
another box and found two
toy poodle dogs who twirled
delicately on their paws.

Just when everyone thought
there could be nothing better,
the toymaker revealed his
Russian dolls.

They danced faster and faster
until everyone was dizzy!

Neither family could decide which dolls to buy.
The toymaker smiled. "In this box," he said,
"I have the most beautiful, the most fabulous
dolls of all."

He opened the lid. Everyone held their breath . . .

There was a pair of dazzling dolls dressed as can-can dancers! They had the most colorful frills and ribbons.

When they danced, it was hard to believe they were only dolls.

"We'll buy them!"
said one family.
"No, we want them!"
said the other family.
They argued and argued
and got very angry.

Ella Bella thought they didn't
deserve such lovely dolls.

"Oh dear," said the toymaker. "Really they belong together, but . . . I suppose I could sell you one each?"

After some more arguing, the families agreed and promised to collect the dolls the next day.

By now it was late. The toymaker closed
the shop and everyone went home.

Everyone, except Ella Bella. She was
worried about the can-can dolls.
How sad they looked, sitting together
by the window.

But then, as the moon rose in the sky, they
slowly began to dance all by themselves . . .

Ella Bella gasped. "Oh, this
is a *magic* toyshop!" she said.

All the other dolls came to life. "Please can you help the can-can dancers?" they asked Ella Bella.

"They are very much in love. It would break their hearts to be parted."

"There are so many boxes," said Ella Bella.
"Perhaps they can hide!"

"Oh, yes!" said the can-can dancers. So Ella Bella
and all the dolls danced around the shop with the
boxes until the can-can dolls were safely hidden.

Soon it was morning, and in came
the toymaker and his apprentice.
Next came the two families.
"We want our dolls!" they demanded.
The toymaker began searching through
his shop, opening this box and that.
"I am sure they are here somewhere . . ."

But, however much he looked,
he could not find them!
The two families started to get angry again.
"I don't understand," said the toymaker.
Just then . . .

. . . all the dolls burst out of the boxes! They knew the toymaker was in trouble.

They danced and clapped and chased both families right out of the shop!

The toymaker began
to laugh. The apprentice
began to laugh. And Ella Bella
laughed, too.

But happiest of all were
the can-can dancers.
"Thank you, Ella Bella!" they cried,
as they twirled around the shop.
"Now we shall stay together always."

The toymaker and his apprentice decided to take the rest of the day off. As Ella Bella danced through the door, the music stopped and she found herself back on the stage.

She gathered up the toys and took them to Madame Rosa.
"Thank you, darling," she said. "Would you like to take a doll home with you?"

"Oh no, thank you," said Ella Bella. "I think they will be much happier if they all stay together."

On her way home, Ella Bella thought about her own dolls. She couldn't wait to tell them about her adventure.

"Who knows," she thought, "one of them might be magical, too!"

# La Boutique Fantasque

There are lots of ballets with dancing toys, like Coppelia and The Nutcracker. But The Magic Toyshop is, perhaps, the most charming of all.

The proper name for this ballet is La Boutique Fantasque, and it was first performed in London by the Ballet Russe company in 1919. The story is set on the French Riviera, in the late 19th century. The scenery was painted by a famous French artist named André Derain.

The music was written by two composers, both from Italy. Gioachino Rossini wrote lots of famous music, including an opera about Cinderella called La Cenerentola. His music is full of sunshine and laughter. After Rossini died, Ottorino Respighi found some piano music by him and thought it would make a lovely ballet. So, he arranged it for a big orchestra, and this made the music very famous. There are all sorts of wonderful tunes, from the Italian Tarantella (a traditional dance inspired by the tarantula spider!), to a dazzling Russian dance and, of course, the French can-can.

Today, the ballet is often performed by dance schools, and because it has just one act, it gives young dancers the perfect opportunity to dance in a full production, and share this enchanting music and magical story with their audience.